SandCastle

Let's Go!

D0103507

LET'S GO

BY

TRUCK

ANDERS HANSON

Consulting Editor, Diane Craig, M.A./Reading Specialist

ABDO Publishing Company

Published by ABDO Publishing Company, 8000 West 78th Street, Edina, MN 55439.

Printed in the United States.

Editor: Pam Price
Curriculum Coordinator: Nancy Tuminelly
Cover and Interior Design and Production: Mighty Media
Photo Credits: Shutterstock

Library of Congress Cataloging-in-Publication Data

Hanson, Anders, 1980-
     Let's go by truck / Anders Hanson.
        p. cm. -- (Let's go!)
     ISBN 978-1-59928-904-5
     1. Trucks--Juvenile literature. I. Title.

TL230.15.H3665 2008
629.224--dc22
                                                                    2007010191

SandCastle™ Level: Transitional

SandCastle™ books are created by a team of professional educators, reading specialists, and content developers around five essential components—phonemic awareness, phonics, vocabulary, text comprehension, and fluency—to assist young readers as they develop reading skills and increase their general knowledge. All books are written, reviewed, and leveled for guided reading, early intervention reading, and Accelerated Reader® programs for use in shared, guided, and independent reading and writing activities to support a balanced approach to literacy instruction. The SandCastle™ series has four levels that correspond to early literacy development. The levels are provided to help teachers and parents select appropriate books for young readers.

Emerging Readers
(no flags)

Beginning Readers
(1 flag)

Transitional Readers
(2 flags)

Fluent Readers
(3 flags)

SandCastle™ would like to hear from you. Please send us your comments or questions.

sandcastle@abdopublishing.com

Trucks travel on roads. They carry heavy goods and large loads.

3

Large trucks are powered by diesel engines.

Big trucks have a lot of tires.

This truck
has a crane.

The biggest trucks are dump trucks.

Taylor visits his
local fire station.
He loves the big,
shiny fire engines.

14

Kara feels tiny inside this huge truck tire!

Ted's dad drives a large earth mover. He lets Ted pretend to drive.

Kyle stands next
to his family's
off-road truck.

HAVE YOU BEEN IN A TRUCK?

WHERE DID YOU GO?

dump truck

garbage truck

pickup truck

semitrailer truck

tank truck

tow truck

The word *truck* comes from the Greek *trochos,* meaning "wheel".

The Liebherr T 282B dump truck has the largest hauling capacity of any truck. It can haul more than 400 tons of goods.

The first truck was built in 1895 by Karl Benz. In 1926, he helped form the Mercedes-Benz company.

GLOSSARY

capacity – the most that something can hold.

crane – a tall machine with cables and a boom arm that is used for moving heavy items.

diesel engine – an engine that runs on diesel fuel.

goods – items that are bought and sold.

semitrailer – a trailer with wheels at the back that is towed by a truck tractor.

To see a complete list of SandCastle™ books and other nonfiction titles from ABDO Publishing Company, visit **www.abdopublishing.com**.

8000 West 78th Street, Edina, MN 55439 • 800-800-1312 • 952-831-1632 fax